Contents

Chapter 1
Pet disasters!

Harry and Ella had longed for a dog of their own and were always pestering their parents to let them have one.

They were given a goldfish instead and this did distract them for a while. They named the fish Jaws, which was not very original, but it was better than Goldy, the name all their friends had chosen for their goldfish (although one had called theirs Sally).

To begin with, the children made themselves dizzy by watching Jaws circle round and round his bowl. They even got excited when he finally swam under the turquoise miniature bridge they had placed in the bottom of the bowl amongst the rainbow gravel.

However, their excitement was not to last as two weeks later Ella found Jaws lying upside down motionless and entangled in the emerald plastic weed.

"I wonder if he died of dizziness." Ella asked.

No one answered her. Later, Dad said he had buried Jaws at the bottom of the garden beneath some bright orange marigolds that grew there. He made the children feel better by telling them that this was the finest place a goldfish could be buried.

Harry was a little suspicious, as he had seen Dad dropping something orange down the toilet and flushing it away!

Initially, they were sad to lose their first ever pet, but spirits were soon lifted by the sight of Mum reluctantly handing over £45 at the local pet shop for a deluxe cage which included a wheel, a play tunnel *and* a Russian hamster. Well, when I say there was a Russian hamster, Harry and Ella had not actually seen him. The pet shop owner told them that Russian hamsters were very shy and often nocturnal. Mum looked anxious at this point, but was reassured that as the hamster became used to them, he would emerge regularly from his hiding place.

Several days later, his existence was confirmed by a tiny pink nose that appeared, twitched several times and then disappeared again.

To make Mum feel better about spending £45, Harry proudly reminded her that she had bought a *Russian* hamster, hoping she would think it was both rare *and* a bargain.

To begin with, the children showed great patience and waited for hours to see if he would appear again. They imagined what it would be like when Boris, as they had named him (Harry thought this sounded Russian), would whizz round on the wheel and scamper through the tunnel playground.

They even invited friends over to keep guard just in case he came out of hiding.

But days passed before he finally flitted out, sniffed the air and scuttled back into the security of his tissue nest. There was just enough time to see a velvety grey coat, little pink toes and jet black eyes.

It was weeks before this largely nocturnal creature braved daylight again and took two steps on the wheel, ignoring his playground completely.

After about six months the children began to get bored of watching and waiting. In fact several days had passed without even the odd twitching of shredded tissue.

The family became concerned and it was

Dad who finally plucked up courage and went to investigate.

He rummaged amongst the tissue and then froze. He looked at Mum and made a face that said, "Get the children out of the room." But Mum believed this was one of those important moments in a child's life and said gently, "No, the children need to see."

Gradually, Dad pulled out by one leg a very stiff and very dead Russian hamster.

He cupped Boris in his hands and both Ella and Harry stroked him gently. They cried a little and there was lots of irritating sniffing, not to mention some ghastly nose-running.

This time the children were determined that Boris was not going

9

to receive the same *flushing* that Jaws had secretly had.

Both stuck like glue to Dad, who was still holding Boris by one stiff little leg. After lots of arguing, it was decided that Boris would be put into a silver tin that they had found in the shed, because the colour matched his fur. He was then buried under a tree in the back garden and the children insisted on saying a prayer together:

> Dear Hamster God,
> Please look after Boris in hamster heaven and give him plenty of toys to play with and a tissue nest to keep him warm.
> Amen

They even tried to read the prayer with a Russian accent as he was a Russian hamster, which made Mum and Dad smile!

Having now lost two beloved pets, Harry and Ella felt they had a better chance of weakening Mum and Dad on the dog issue. So again they began to pester their parents and they used every trick in the 'pestering book'.

First, they used both sad and angelic faces, but that got them nowhere. Then they tried voices that sounded as if they were on the edge of tears.

"I hardly ever ask for anything," lied Ella, who was constantly asking for things!

However, Mum and Dad weren't moved one bit. They even laughed!

Finally, Harry and Ella both thought it was time for the technique that usually worked when everything else failed.

Ella went first, waving her school report in the air and reminding Mum and Dad that she had got loads of Level 5s in her SATs.

Harry quickly followed by holding up his certificates for winning the 100-metre sprint and the three-legged race at the school sports day.

This tactic didn't seem to be working, so they both hurtled upstairs and came back down wearing their Brownie and Cub uniforms.

"Oh, look!" said Harry smugly. "I've got my new Animal carer and Home safety badges on."

"Oh, would you believe it?" said Ella in the same voice. "I seem to have got my new Book lover and Friend to animals badges."

For a moment, it looked like the word 'yes' was right on the tip of Dad's tongue.

But no, it was not to be as all Dad said was, "You don't do something to get something," in a really annoying 'grown-ups know best' voice.

To make matters worse, Mum then chipped in with reasons why not to have a dog.

"It needs lots of exercise and you will soon get tired of taking it for walks."

"We won't, we won't," the children said, jumping up and down.

"They moult and their hair gets everywhere!" added Mum.

In response to this, Ella grabbed a brush from the kitchen and started brushing the furniture, whilst Harry started to vacuum the carpet!

"Stop it," laughed Mum. "You're being ridiculous!" she chuckled.

"They'll poo in the garden," Dad then added.

"I'll pick it up," Harry promised.

"Well, *I'm* not," said an ever stubborn Ella under her breath.

"And wee! Think of the plants and grass," said Mum, making it sound even worse.

"Well, I'll take it out and make it stand in one place on some soil," offered Ella, not knowing how she was going to actually do it.

At this point, Harry ruined everything.

"Everyone else has got a dog!" he announced in desperation.

Well, that was it.

"End of discussion and go and do your homework," ordered Dad.

Ella was furious with Harry and argued with him all the way up the stairs, then slammed her bedroom door.

However, a very stern **"Ella!"** from Dad downstairs meant she had to open it and close it again quietly.

Chapter 2
Hour by hour

What happened next is a mystery. Was it Mum who was overheard saying to Dad in their bedroom, "Well, they've lost both a fish and a hamster." Or was it Dad who was heard in the kitchen saying, "They're good children, you know, and we could take it back if it goes wild."

Something had changed in their parents' minds and the children were summoned to the front room and told to sit down a minute. Harry and Ella looked at each other nervously, as this was what usually happened when they were about to be told off or given a lecture. The last time it happened was when Harry had put black shoe polish on the black toilet seats in the boys' toilets at school. Before that, it was the time when Ella had deliberately coughed (and it was a wet dribbly one!) over Carrianne's cupcakes when she refused to let her have one. But on this occasion, neither of them could think of anything bad they had done.

"You can stop looking like that," said Dad, with a smirk on his face. "This is one of the few times you are *not* in trouble!"

"Phew," the children said together.

"Your mother and I," Dad began. (Boy, this must be important as Dad had never used *that* phrase.) "Your mother and I have had a long talk."

(Get on with it, the children both thought. The suspense is killing us!)

"We have decided ..."

He paused on purpose to make the wait more agonising.

"... that you can have a dog."

The announcement was greeted with total silence as Harry and Ella were in such a state of shock that their jaws had jammed. Harry finally stuttered in disbelief.

"P-P-Pardon?"

"You can have a dog," Mum confirmed.

At this point hysteria broke out!

Ella screamed her way around the whole house, visiting every room, including the toilet, the broom cupboard, under the stairs and the front porch.

Harry simultaneously punched his fists in the air, repeating the words "Yes, yes, yes!" as he circled the garden endlessly.

Dad kept shouting for them to calm down, but it was pointless. Ella, by this time, was cartwheeling in and out of the kitchen and Harry had rushed into the street and was telling everyone he met, including complete strangers, that they were having a dog.

After an hour, calm finally returned to their house, well a kind of calm. Both children could be seen at the front door with coats and shoes on and wearing backpacks containing ginger nut biscuits wrapped in cling film as a dog treat. Ella also had a skipping rope inside her backpack just in case they needed a lead.

Harry then remembered something and

rushed upstairs. He came back with a tartan picnic blanket so the dog had something to snuggle up on in the back of the car.

"Where do you think you two are going?" enquired Mum.

"To get the dog," they replied together.

"We're not going now," declared Mum grinning. "Probably Saturday, but no promises."

"Oh," said Harry like a sulky teenager.

"That's ages," whined Ella.

"Well, you'll have to be patient," Mum told them firmly.

They both stomped upstairs like two lazy elephants and slumped onto their beds defeated.

Saturday was nearly five whole days away. Harry had worked out that it was actually 117 hours away or 7,020 minutes or 421,200 seconds, to be really precise. The amount of minutes and seconds made the children utterly depressed, so they stuck to hours.

Ella drew up a chart to tick off each hour as it passed. At the bottom it said 'Saturday, 9 o'clock' as this was when they had decided it was dog collecting time!

By Wednesday, they realised that counting hours was making things worse because time was taking so long to pass.

A different strategy was needed, so they started to keep busy.

Harry tidied up his bedroom, which rarely

happened, and he offered to hang out the washing and mow the lawn. To Mum and Dad's astonishment, he even baked some cupcakes! They looked delicious, but tasted revolting. But that didn't seem to matter.

Ella asked to paint her bedroom walls, which made Mum and Dad very nervous. Dad helped by doing the finishing touches and they both agreed the end result was acceptable, even if they didn't particularly like the shade of pink she had chosen.

Second by second, hour by hour, the days passed and Saturday finally arrived!

Neither child had difficulty getting up, but they were sent back to bed by a very angry Dad, who had heard crunching noises and was furious to discover both children eating cornflakes for breakfast at 3 o'clock in the morning!

Mum and Dad eventually caved into pressure, well, more like exhaustion, and at 8.30 precisely, they all clambered into the car to head for the Dog Rescue Centre.

Chapter 3
D-day!

Mum nearly lost her temper after Ella and Harry had asked "Are we there yet?" around twenty times. In fact, Harry had actually started to ask after only a quarter of a mile into the journey.

They were ordered to sit in silence, making it one of the longest and most torturous journeys of their lives.

It was even longer, Ella thought, than the school trip to the zoo, during which the coach had been forced to stop five times to let Tracey Adams get off and be sick on the verge.

Sadly on the first occasion she didn't quite make it and shot sick all over the back of the driver's seat. The smell that then wafted around the bus made Karl Ingram throw up all over Derek Patterson's lap. He'd been sucking blackcurrant sweets so it looked decidedly purple!

"There it is!" pointed Dad.

These were the words that both children had waited 421,000 plus seconds for!

They stretched their seatbelts to the limit to peer through the front windscreen. And there indeed it was, the place they had dreamed about for days. Hanging above a set of tall burgundy metal gates was a large white sign with Dog Rescue Centre written on it.

Behind the gates, a long driveway led towards rows and rows of small rectangular buildings, fronted with wire-netted wooden frames.

"Those must be the kennels," said Harry excitedly.

"But I can't see any dogs," added Ella anxiously.

"Don't worry, I expect they're inside," replied Mum reassuringly.

Dad led the way to the front office. The noise was deafening, as it seemed hundreds of dogs were barking at once. Big deep woofs, continuous yaps, wolf-like howls and a few snarls all blended into one great din!

"This is like the bit in *101 Dalmatians* when all the dogs across the town and country bark to each other," shouted Ella, holding her hands over her ears.

They were met in the office by a lady wearing a burgundy sweatshirt with 'Dog Rescue Centre' embroidered on the front of it. Her name was Daphne. She had a warm welcoming smile, the kind that made the children know she was caring and that they were going to like her.

They just hoped she was going to like *them*! As she began to tell them that there were 167 dogs to be viewed, the children hid shyly behind their parents. Secretly they were at bursting point and could hardly wait to see the dogs.

However, they would have to wait a little

longer for that moment as there were forms to be filled in and lots and lots of questions to answer:

"Have you had a dog before?"

"What is your house like?"

"Have you got a garden?"

"How old are the children?"

"Have you had any pets at all?"

To which Harry replied, "A short-lived goldfish and a hamster we only ever saw properly five times!"

Mum made one of her faces which meant the children were to be seen and not heard.

Ella ignored this face and decided to chip in proudly.

"It was a *Russian* hamster!"

Then she wished she hadn't opened her mouth as she felt her face go bright red and she quickly darted behind Dad.

After filling in two more forms and showing a gas bill to prove the family's address, the children thought the moment they had so longed for had finally arrived.

But, they were about to be hugely disappointed. Daphne brought out an enormous photo album for the family to view.

"Don't we go and see the dogs now?" asked Ella in desperation.

Daphne explained that many of the dogs get very excited and others very nervous when visitors arrive. If they let the general public in constantly, it would not be good for them. So reluctantly the children began to turn the pages of the album. Each page had several photos of each dog and then lots of details about them.

"Alfie loves long walks."

"Trixie hates postmen and postwomen."

"Amber has been known to run off."

"Tiger is a very shy dog."

Suddenly, the children were in doggy heaven! It was like a dog sweet shop! There were dogs of every kind. Small ones, huge ones, round ones, thin ones, long ones, hairy ones and smooth ones.

Then there were all sorts of doggy ears: pointed, floppy, furry and hairy. When it came to tails, some were curly, others straight, lots of waggy-looking ones and some dogs had almost no tail at all.

One dog had a coat that looked like the mat in the toilet at home and another had so much hair you couldn't see its face!

The children had never seen so many patterns, with spotty dogs, patchy dogs and almost every colour imaginable. There was blonde, chocolate, charcoal, ginger, ash, and colours that the children had never even heard of, like brindle and liver!

Things got even more complicated when Daphne began to tell them the breeds of the pedigree dogs. Some were easy like Labrador, Bulldog and Greyhound, which the children knew. But some you could hardy pronounce like Bichon Frise and Dandie Dinmont! Then there were the dogs she called mongrels and Daphne explained they were a mixture of breeds. Each dog also had a pet name. Some had arrived with one, but the others were given one by the Dog Rescue Centre staff. There was Buddy, Coco, Winston, Rusty, Basil, Shadow, Princess, Samson, Sasha, Ted, Patch, Dixie, Roxie and even Tootsie and Splat!

After lots of discussion and help from Mum and Dad, a shortlist of dogs was made. This had not been an easy task as Harry and Ella had chosen every dog in the centre to start with because they had all been gorgeous, cute, cuddly or adorable!

"Right," said a relieved Daphne, "let's go and see your shortlist!"

The family then moved on in a slightly calmer fashion from one kennel to the next. In some, they were greeted by the waggiest of tails imaginable and in others by endless barking. Then there were the sad dogs who hid in corners and shivered like Harry and Ella did after outdoor swimming lessons at the Lido pool. As they passed each kennel, one of the children would say, "That one!" But as soon as they got to the next kennel, it

would change to "No, this one."

"You can't have them all, just one!" said Mum, who was beginning to despair at the whole process of choosing a dog.

"Right, decision time," said Dad firmly, as he could sense Mum was 'on the edge'.

Harry and Ella looked at each other. Harry had that dizzy look on his face like he had had when he had sneaked into the kitchen last Boxing Day and had drunk some cider. They all took one more look at the shortlist of dogs.

Would it be the one whose tongue licked them endlessly through the wire netting? Or perhaps the little dog with three spots on his bottom?

One by one they each said they had decided. They were just about to announce their decision when they heard a deep woof, deeper than any they had heard so far. It came from behind a green wooden door at the far end of the kennel house.

"Who's that?" asked Harry.

"Oh, that dog only came in last week. He

has needed a bit longer to settle in than usual. He hasn't even got a name yet," Daphne informed them.

"Can we see him?" asked Mum gently. She had an unusual look on her face.

"Well, he's a bit frisky really," said Daphne.

"*Please*," pleaded Ella, as if she knew something too.

Daphne took one look at their faces and weakened.

"Come on then, let's take a quick peep," she whispered. "But I really shouldn't do this, it's against regulations."

They walked the long length of the kennels, remembering not to disturb the dogs as they passed by.

"Why is he behind here and not in the kennels with the others?" asked Dad.

"Well, we've had to put him in a special kennel as he keeps escaping," Daphne explained.

Behind the door was a large kennel, higher than all the others with much thicker wire netting and a dull metal floor.

And there he was, the dog with no name, sitting waiting with a look on his face which seemed to say, "I knew you would find me!" And what a dog he was!

Chapter 4
This one!

The first thing that everyone noticed was his huge paws!

"Those paws are the size of a lion's," gasped Harry.

Then there was his nose. It was heart-shaped like a polar bear's, with large round nostrils.

"What breed is he?" asked Dad.

"Good question," laughed Daphne. "I don't think we have ever seen a dog with so many breeds in it. His paws could be a Great Dane's and his nose is like a Saint Bernard's. As for his tail, it's probably a bit of Golden Retriever. And his colours, well, your guess is as good as mine," she sighed.

It was as if someone had gone a little wild with a doggy paintbrush. One paw was white, two were black and the last one chocolate brown. One ear was grey and stuck up, the other one was white and flopped down.

His tail was white, too, and very hairy. The rest of him was a hotchpotch of all the different shades.

"Where did he come from?" asked Dad.

"He was found wandering in a park. He had very muddy paws, no microchip, no collar and he was very, very hungry. We think he had been abandoned, and by his condition, he'd been on his own for some time," Daphne told them.

Everyone looked sad at this point, but the dog with no name didn't look sad. He paced up and down wagging his tail wildly as if he was at Crufts, showing himself at his best.

Daphne began to turn away saying, "I think we may have trouble finding a family for this one and we may have to ...," but she didn't finish the sentence. She quickly changed the subject and asked the family which dog it was going to be.

"THIS ONE," they all said together.

"Which one?" she asked again.

"This one!" they all confirmed.

A wonderful glowing feeling surrounded the whole family. Rarely did they all agree on something.

"Well, you do know he's a handful," warned Daphne.

"Yes," replied Dad, so confidently that Mum held his hand proudly.

"He needs us and we need him," he said.

Well, this sealed the deal. By this point, Mum and both children had tears rolling down their cheeks.

"Do you need my skipping rope?" blubbered Ella.

"What for?" asked Mum.

"For his lead," she answered.

"We can't take him today," Mum told her.

Her words were followed by a long
"Oooooh!" from Ella and at least four tuts
from Harry.

"He'll also need to have his injections
against diseases and we'll need to de-flea him.
He's got lots," Daphne added.

That information was enough to change
the children's minds and they realised he
wasn't quite ready to go home with them yet.
Both children had caught nits at school, so
they were a little sensitive about tiny
creepy-crawlies.

Amazingly, none of this seemed to put anyone off, even Mum and Dad still looked determined that this dog was the one.

"We'll need to visit your home to check it's suitable for a dog this size," Daphne told them.

Harry's mind was already spinning, thinking of all the things that needed to be moved! The slide and swing would have to go. Anyway, no one ever played on them now. Perhaps the trampoline would need to go, too.

At this point, the dog's face seemed to change as if he sensed that they weren't going to take him, but Harry and Ella quickly comforted him.

"We'll be back soon," they both promised.

He licked their fingers through the wire as if he understood.

On the way home, no one could stop talking, especially as Daphne had said if all went well, it may only take a month before he could be coming home with them!

Chapter 5
Mum knows best!

The weeks that followed were agonising. The days just seemed to drag on, but there was some brief excitement when Cindy, another lady from the Dog Rescue Centre, gave the house a thorough check and said it seemed perfect! The children squealed with delight and rushed down the street to tell all their friends.

They then attended all the training sessions at the Dog Rescue Centre and it was as if the dog knew he had to be on his best behaviour. Even Daphne was surprised at how well they were all bonding.

Mum and Dad felt they could now buy some doggy things and frequent trips to pet shops helped the time to pass.

They bought far too much, of course. A huge basket bed, three dog rugs, two sets of plastic food bowls and a metal one for water. Then there were several brushes for every occasion, an extending long lead and a short one too, 24 tins of dog food, five sacks of the dried version just in case he didn't like the wet sort, doggy nibbles for treats, a bag of 100 poo bags, a pooper scooper and lots of dog toys.

As Harry had predicted, the swing, the slide and, yes, even the trampoline, had to go, but they all went to a good home. The children next door had longed for their own playground and now they had an instant ready-assembled one.

Dad also decided the greenhouse was a definite no-no for a large lively dog so Uncle Phil came over and helped him take it down. That too went to a good home as Aunty Emma had been desperate for one.

Mum made space in the utility room for the dog basket, although the children had foolishly thought they would be taking turns having the dog sleep in their bedrooms.

She also moved anything fragile and placed ornaments on high shelves.

Dad constructed a fence, again with the help of Uncle Phil (who always seemed to be so clever with his hands on these occasions), which completely surrounded his pride and joy, the vegetable patch. The children busied themselves checking there were no gaps in the big garden fence that a dog could squeeze under and they dug up a small patch of turf where the dog with no name could wee.

As for names for the dog without one, hundreds of possibilities were suggested throughout the weeks. They ranged from Curly (because of his tail), Big Foot and Nosey (for obvious reasons) to Samson, based on his size, Rainbow, as he seemed to have so many colours in his coat, and Joseph (who was in the Bible and had a coat of many colours too!).

Then followed doggy-type names like Buster, Bruno, Spike, Lucky, Max, Rocky, Duke, Butch, Dexter and Barney. Exhaustion set in as the weeks went by and the children began to suggest ridiculous names like Stink, Sausage, Meatball and Boo Boo. The worst name of all was chosen by Dad.

"Let's call him Puddles, seeing as that's what he'll make lots of," he joked.

Things got so silly that they decided to wait until the dog arrived to choose the perfect name.

When that Saturday did finally come, even Mum and Dad seemed excited. They had rushed breakfast and were at the Dog Rescue Centre before it had even opened its gates. "You're keen," Daphne laughed through the car window!

Harry carried the long lead and Ella carried the short one, while Dad fastened the dog guard behind the two back seats and Mum laid out a blanket in the boot ready for the new member of their family.

The children, who had been almost uncontrollably excited on the journey and were still arguing over names, could hardly wait to get into the Centre.

"He's in the departure kennel where all our dogs spend their last night," Daphne told them.

She then showed them the way and there he was, tail quivering, endlessly woofing and so excited that he appeared to be prancing like a circus horse.

"Don't go in," said Daphne. "Just talk to him gently and get to know each other some more."

She then went off and signed the final

paperwork. Dad handed over a donation cheque to help the Centre rescue other dogs.

By the time they all arrived back, the dog with no name was nuzzling against the wire mesh and licking the children's fingers.

Daphne went into the kennel first and gave the dog lots of pats and hugs. She then got him to lie on the floor and rubbed his tummy, which he really seemed to like. At this point, she beckoned to the children to come in slowly and sit alongside her.

The children joined in the tummy-rubbing. He seemed to adore this and nearly licked them to death. The more the children giggled,

the more he licked them. Mum and Dad joined them and Daphne slipped out of the kennel and watched from behind the mesh, with the broadest grin on her face. She knew she was looking at instant love between a dog and a family.

Eventually, they were nearly sore by all the licking, so Daphne decided it was time to put the lead on the dog.

It was at this very moment, as the family would often remember in the years ahead, that a new life of adventure began. As the lead clicked on, the dog took flight with Harry clinging like a limpet to the end of it.

Out he went, through the kennels and into the exercise area, whizzing round and round in endless circuits like a moth round a light!

It was as if they had forgotten all the training tips they had been given on their visits to the Centre.

"Don't worry," said Daphne. "This regularly happens on the first day!" she said, reassuringly.

Harry refused to let go even though everyone was shouting at him to do so. He was determined to show the dog who was boss.

After about ten minutes, the dog did finally give in and flopped down panting.

Harry felt like a rodeo rider who had calmed a bucking bronco horse, although he was too tired to fully celebrate.

Daphne then took hold of the lead and led a now exhausted dog to the family car. But that was far from the end of the trouble.

The dog had clearly never been in a car before and wasn't about to without a struggle. He sat down and simply refused to move!

They tried every approach. They dragged, they pushed and they attempted to lift! They even tied a scarf over his eyes, but nothing worked.

"Wait a minute," said Ella. "I've got a cereal bar in my pocket." She scrambled into the back of the car, unwrapped the bar and waved it through the dog guard that Dad had been lent by the Rescue Centre. The dog smelt it instantly with his big nose and after two sniffs in the air, leapt forward and bit half the bar off in one go. No sooner on board, Dad slammed down the hatch and the dog was in!

What followed was not pleasant. Suddenly frightened, the dog panicked, began scratching frantically at the glass and woofed continuously. Daphne could see he was distressed.

"We'd better let him out," she told them.

By the time Dad opened the hatch, the dog had weed on one of the blankets, making the eventual journey home a smelly one. So they were back to square one!

"Just a minute! I have another idea," said Mum in one of those Mum voices that always sounds as if everything will be alright.

"Get into the back, children, and snuggle up either side of the other blanket," she instructed.

She then led the dog to the open side door of the car and let him just sniff and look.

After a short pause, the dog took a huge leap over Ella and flopped down between her and Harry and laid his head gently on Harry's lap.

His tail quivered in Ella's face, making her laugh almost hysterically.

"Brilliant!" shouted Daphne enthusiastically.

"You brainbox," said Dad, as he kissed Mum on the cheek.

"Call it a mum's intuition," she smirked.

"'Mums know best,' they always say."

And she was right on this occasion.

All the dog needed was a cuddle and this was how he would always travel in the car.

They thanked Daphne, waved goodbye and set off for home.

"One of my staff will be over in a week or so to see how things are going," she shouted.

The dog let out his loudest woof yet as if to say, "Thanks for everything, but here's to a new life!"

Chapter 6
Bull in a china shop!

Getting the dog into the car was nothing compared to what they faced once they got home.

Dad got out of the car first and opened the front door of the house. That was the biggest mistake. As soon as Ella opened the car door, the dog was gone faster than a fighter jet and disappeared into the house in a flash.

By the time anyone could get inside, all they could do was stand and watch helplessly.

The dog was darting from room to room, up the stairs, down the stairs, over and over again.

Things fell, flew and were flung.

The dog bumped, bashed and banged his way through every inch of the house.

He went over, under and inside every nook and cranny!

This would have gone on a lot longer, had it not been for the various items he began to collect.

First, a long, knitted, orange scarf that had been hanging on some coat hooks wrapped itself around one of the dog's back legs.

Next, a patterned throw from the sofa twisted its way around the dog's belly.

Finally, a clothes dryer was knocked over and Dad's tiger stripe underpants landed on the dog's head, covering his eyes.

What followed resembled a game of Ring-a-ring-a-roses as the dog spun round and round until he fell down exhausted and panting.

By this time, the house looked like it had been burgled. Nothing was in its place and almost everything in the bedrooms and front room had been knocked over.

No one said a word, as they just looked at the mess and then at each other.

Mum broke the silence.

"Oh no, not my porcelain ornament!" she moaned. (The ornament was a wedding present! It was a clown holding balloons.)

"What have we done?" whispered a shocked Dad.

Then a large nose appeared from beneath Dad's pants and two ears popped through each leg hole. The dog seemed to have the ability to just look at them and twitch his nose or blink with his long eyelashes and the family would melt and fall back in love with him.

"Oh, it's just a clown," said Mum forgivingly.

Then they set off tidying up, repairing and, sadly, throwing away.

In total, the dog managed to break twelve ornaments, two mirrors, a clock, a vase, three pictures and a glass thermometer.

He had flattened a huge dried flower

display, crushed Ella's doll's house and managed to destroy two shelf units.

Harry imagined that this was what the phrase 'like a bull in a china shop' meant.

Whilst the house was being put back together, the dog lay still, flashing his two huge eyelashes. This made him look totally angelic and adorable.

"That dog knows exactly how to win us over," chuckled Dad.

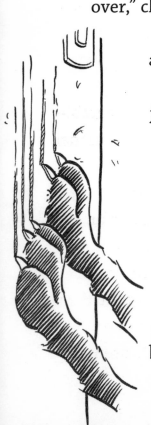

The family began talking about a new name for him again.

"How about Crashbangwallop?" joked Dad.

"No, Smashalot!" suggested Harry.

"Or Tornado," Mum giggled.

Perhaps the dog sensed he was being made fun of because he began to scratch the floor by the back door. Then he started to scratch the door itself and, boy, could he scratch!

Within minutes, the floor and door were covered in deep grooves created by the dog's long nails.

"Let him out," screamed Mum, "before he completely ruins the door!"

Dad opened the door and out the dog tore, like a stallion released into the wild. He raced in circles, leapt in the air and twisted and turned from one direction to another. At one point it looked as if he was dancing like those performing dogs that appear on TV.

He then explored every inch of the garden, sniffing in each corner and under every plant. He stared longingly at Dad's vegetable patch where the new fence prevented further mayhem.

Then he was off again, darting and pouncing across the lawn as if chasing an imaginary mouse or grasshopper.

Finally, he paused by one of Mum's rose bushes. It was a red one called Fragrant Cloud. Dad had bought it for Mum one Valentine's Day. The dog sniffed its scent.

"Oh no," yelled Mum. "Quickly, someone grab his lead. I know exactly what he's going to do!"

Harry and Ella ran as quickly as they could, but it was too late. A cocked leg was followed by the largest wee either of the children had ever seen all over the rose.

"That's the end of that one," sighed Mum in resignation.

"No, don't be silly, one wee won't kill it," said Dad. But a month later he was proved wrong.

Now that the children were in the garden, it was fun and games time for the dog.

He played Chase, Follow the leader, Hide and seek and, finally, Knock you over, at which point Dad intervened because the dog was getting too rough.

So the children sat on the step and just admired the dog they adored.

Suddenly, he stopped exploring and began to sniff the air.

"What can he smell?" asked Harry.

"Your feet probably," Ella joked.

"No, look, he's caught a scent," he whispered.

"Hope it's not a rat," shivered Ella.

The dog had indeed caught a scent. At the front of the house, Dad was unloading dog food into the garage and the dog could smell food from miles away!

As soon as Dad entered the kitchen, he was pounced on.

If it hadn't been for Mum and the two children who managed to pull the dog off,

Dad would have probably been eaten too!

"Boy, this dog has a good nose!"
declared Mum.

Wherever Dad tried to hide the food, the dog found it.

Finally, in desperation, Dad put the food in the boot of the car outside.

Not only did the dog have a good sense of smell, he also had an appetite to match it. He was always hungry. For his first meal, he ate two large tins of dog food, three bowls of dried mix and five bone-shaped biscuits. And still he looked for more!

As bedtime approached, Harry and Ella made up the dog's bed. They placed two tartan blankets inside a wicker basket and set out his toys next to it. They filled up his metal bowl with water and then proceeded to say night, night at least twenty times.

"Right, bed now," growled Mum.

Mum and Dad soon followed and even they said night, night five times!

Dad closed the kitchen door nervously,

fearing what other mess he might find in the morning.

The house lights had only been out for minutes when a commotion could be heard in Harry's bedroom.

The dog had decided there was no way he was going to be left alone. Somehow he had opened both the kitchen and bedroom doors.

When Mum and Dad got to the bedroom, they found the dog lying on top of Harry, who was pinned down like a wrestler and laughing fit to burst.

The dog was removed firmly and given his marching orders as he was banished back to the kitchen.

Dad then placed a chair against the door to barricade the dog in.

Lights again went out. Minutes later, there was another commotion, but this time from Ella's bedroom.

Mum and Dad were greeted by what looked like a tent. The dog had got under the duvet and had curled up next to a hysterical little girl.

"Right," said Dad, with a voice that sounded like he meant business.

The dog was given his marching orders again and banished back to the kitchen. This time, Dad wedged a broom handle between the door and wall. He even put a further wooden wedge at its base.

Then for good measure, he put a heavier chair against the door.

"Get that open," thought Dad smugly.

Lights went out yet again. But then the

barking began!

"Ignore it," shouted Dad.

So everyone did their best. Ella put her head under the pillow while Harry wrapped his football scarf around his head.

Dad bent his pillow around his head to cover each ear!

"This is torture," groaned Mum. "It's worse than the children's pop music!"

"Ignore it," repeated Dad grumpily. But ignore it you couldn't, as it went on and on and on.

"Think of the neighbours," pleaded Mum.

Dad finally caved in and marched downstairs.

He got even crosser at having to remove wedges and chairs.

Soon he was greeted by a dog whose tail was vibrating faster than ever and had the most innocent face imaginable.

Dad was just about to yell at the top of his voice, but melted instantly and could only manage a feeble "You!"

By this time, the whole family had gathered at the door.

"Oh, look at him," Mum said, going all gooey!

"Well, he's not going in the bedrooms, and that's final," said Dad firmly.

After much discussion, the dog basket was placed on the landing.

The lights went out yet again and everyone lay nervously, waiting to see what would happen next. Apart from the odd snuffle and several snorts, there was silence, blissful silence, because the dog had clearly only wanted to be close to the family.

Chapter 7
Poo!

This closeness, however, was to be tested to the limit some hours later as the dog was an early riser. At 5 o'clock in the morning, to be precise! The morning began with a muffled woof, followed by a pitiful whimper, two howls and then the full works of continuous deep barking.

The children were already awake, longing to get up and see their adorable new dog.

Bravely, Harry called to Mum and Dad.

"I think he wants a wee. Can I let him out?" he asked.

A grunt from Dad was all Harry and Ella needed. They hurtled downstairs and opened the back door.

The dog circled the garden, sniffing.

"That's what dogs do when they need a wee!" Harry informed Ella, as if he was a dog

63

expert. But he was proved to be wrong as it was not a wee he wanted first, it was a poo.

And *what a poo*!

The children stood with open mouths in shock as the poo just kept coming.

"Wow!" gasped Ella. "What a pile!"

The dog kicked backwards several times, sending tufts of grass into the air and then proceeded to wee at several locations around the garden.

Once the job was done, he trotted happily back indoors.

Mum had now shuffled downstairs. Once she was awake, she could never stay in bed.

"What's up with you two?" she yawned.

"Mum, look, it's enormous!" declared Ella.

"What is?" asked Mum.

"Come and look," said Harry.

"Wow, that *is* a big one. He really did need to go!" chuckled Mum. "Well, get on with it," she ordered.

"Get on with what?" asked Ella.

"Remember your promise?" she reminded them.

The colour drained from both children's faces as they suddenly remembered that they had promised to scoop up all poo!

"Can you do this one?" pleaded Harry.

"Nope," Mum said, shaking her head.

"Oh, go on. This one is too big for children," he whimpered.

"A promise is a promise. Or shall we take the dog back to the Rescue Centre?"

The children quickly collected two poo bags (just in case) and the scooper and made their way gingerly towards the mound of poo that was now steaming gently.

Twice they stopped en route and whispered things like "This is awful", "I can't do it", "I feel sick" and "If *you* do it, *I* will clean your bedroom for a year!"

But when a job has to be done, a job has to be done.

Dad had joined Mum. Both were laughing so much it hurt. The dog watched too, confused by all the fuss.

Twice the children gagged as if they were going to be sick and then decided it was best to do the job as quickly as possible.

Ella held the bag open and Harry plunged the scooper into the steaming pile. One, two, three, four, five attempts were needed before it had all gone.

They both ran as fast as lightning towards the dustbin.

"No, you don't," called Dad. "You've got to tie the top first." Ella said she just couldn't and nearly cried, so Harry did what a brother has to sometimes do and knotted the bag quicker than a boy scout could.

They both ran indoors and washed their hands several times. Thankfully, this task was going to get easier over time, but never something they would like doing.

"Right, an early breakfast, I think," chirped Dad. "Chocolate spread on toast would be nice!"

Both children groaned and decided not to have any breakfast at all.

Chapter 8
Walkies!

Later that day, after lots of nagging from the children, Dad agreed they could take their dog for his first walk. The children were desperate to show him off to their friends in the street, but things did not go as planned.

It was more of a tug of war with the dog on one side and Mum, Dad and both children on the other.

What must the neighbours have thought seeing one dog dragging four people at an ever-increasing speed down the street and several times around a lamp post?

It looked like the worst ever example of May Pole dancing, and it left them all totally entangled.

In fact, if it hadn't been for Mr Jefferson from number 24, they may have still been there! He kindly clung to the dog while the family, who by this point were feeling totally embarrassed, untangled themselves.

Things eventually got a little better, but Dad wouldn't let the children hold the dog on their own.

They also discovered that he had an irritating habit that stayed with him all his life. He weed all the time. Not one long wee. No! Short ones at every lamp post, fence, gate, bush, tree, rock and patch of grass. More embarrassing was his tendency to also wee on car wheels and in doorways.

A walk with this dog became one long string of apologies.

To the relief of the family, they finally reached the open fields at the end of their estate.

This was the children's paradise playground. It was here that they spent most of their free time. It was particularly safe as the local houses overlooked the fields and no main roads had to be crossed to reach them.

It was here that Harry and Ella regularly

made dens, collected conkers, blew dandelions, rode their BMX bikes over humps and bumps, and waded through boggy swamps when it rained.

The family stood on the edge of the fields, all thinking the same thing.

"Should we let him off his lead?"

One of three things could happen.

He would run off and never come back, he would run off and take ages to come back or he would scamper off and play, but keep close to the family.

He was such a big active dog that none of the family could bear to think he would always have to stay on his lead. (They were also thinking how sore their hands and arms were already.)

There was only one way to find out.

They all crossed fingers and toes and held their breaths as Dad unclipped the lead.

For a brief moment, the dog paused, unable to believe he could leave them. Then he bounded off, leaping about like a young deer.

"Oh no," cried Dad, "we haven't given him a name. How are we going to get him back?"

"We'll whistle," said Mum confidently.

To everyone's total surprise and huge relief, Dad gave one whistle and the dog bounded back.

They could hardly believe it. In fact each time they whistled, he came back and then set off again.

"Well, his previous owner must have taught him something, thank goodness," sighed Mum.

Everyone now felt comfortable to let him have some freedom to explore the spaces and places the children loved to play in.

He must have sniffed every inch of the area. The children climbed a nearby tree while Mum and Dad sat on a bench, exhausted from the previous tug of war.

After a while, they lost sight of him behind tall grass, so the children set off to investigate what he was up to.

As they approached, they could see soil

flying into the air like a mud fountain.

When they finally reached the dog, they could hardly believe their eyes. The dog stopped briefly, quivered his tail wildly and then continued to dig a huge hole big enough for him and both the children to climb into.

"Mum, Dad, come quickly!" called Ella.

There was no stopping the dog. Now that he had an audience, he dug faster and faster, deeper and deeper.

"Wow!" Mum and Dad said together.

"It's those big paws of his," said Ella.

"He's like a JCB digger!" Harry added in amazement.

Dad decided it was time to stop him before he ruined the field. But stopping him proved much more difficult than expected. It took all four of them heaving the lead together.

"This is like in *Indiana Jones and the Temple of Doom* when the rope bridge collapses and they have to heave Indiana up the cliff," groaned Harry.

Four against one eventually proved too much and after a few gentle growls, the dog gave in and followed them home. On the way back, the friends of the family now had a chance to see the new dog.

All the way along the street there were lots of pats, hugs, strokes, the odd kiss and "Aahs", "Wows", and "Oh, he's so cute".

Almost everyone who stopped to say hello got licked to death too.

Once at home, the children played a game of Hunt the dog biscuit, which was like Hunt the thimble, but with biscuits.

They couldn't believe how good the dog was. Wherever they hid the biscuits, he found them in seconds. Even when Dad hid them in a tin, inside another tin, inside a plastic bag in a box on the top shelf in the shed, he went straight to them!

"This dog is simply amazing," declared Harry. "I know. Let's call him Sniffer!"

But not everyone agreed.

"It sounds like he's got a cold," laughed Ella.

"Or a runny nose," added Mum.

"What about Sniff?" asked Dad.

These were followed by other suggestions like Snuffle, Whiff and even Smelly, all of which were quickly rejected.

More work was definitely needed on the dog-naming!

Chapter 9
Bubbles!

After several outings to the fields, during which time he would always dig, and after a lot of time spent in the garden, the dog was in need of a bath.

Not only was he grubby but, boy, did he smell!

"I think he's rolled in something nasty," snorted Ella, as she held her nose.

Many dogs love to have a bath, but would this one?

In recent days, Dad had begun to get on everyone's nerves as he had suddenly become a dog expert. He had been reading a book called *Getting to Know a Man's Best Friend: Living Happily with your Dog*. What particularly drove everyone mad was that he insisted on quoting from it.

This awful book seemed to give advice on

everything from feeding to grooming, and it even had a smell chart giving the levels of how smelly your dog may get.

Doggy smell
(to be expected)

A bit pongy
(it is beginning to make the house smell)

WOW! Stinky
(time to put the dog out in the garden)

What's that stench?
(time to take your dog to the beauty parlour!)

By now, Dad was in full flow and felt the need to read out the eight stages of bathing a dog.

"One. Buy shampoo.

Two. Shower the dog completely from head to toe.

Three. Squirt a bit of shampoo on your hands.

Four. Rub it into the dog's fur.

Five. Rinse.

Six. Repeat.

Seven. Let your dog shake.
Eight. Dry with a towel."

Everyone groaned.

"This is so obvious," Mum moaned.

"If a job is going to be done, it must be done properly," said Dad, in one of his aggravatingly know-it-all voices.

What followed allowed Mum and the children to smirk annoyingly for the rest of the day.

Dad headed towards the dog, who was sitting innocently on the lawn, with a long green hose.

But this dog had seen a hose before and knew exactly what it meant. He shot inside the house.

The children found him hiding under a bed. He was dragged back for a second attempt, but this time managed to exhaust Dad by darting and leaping all around the garden, much to everyone's delight.

"Right, we'll have to do this in the

bathroom where he can't get out!" said Dad.

Mum and the children looked at each other with eyes wide open. They knew that this was going to be fun!

"Dad's going to get soaked hopefully," Harry whispered naughtily.

The poor dog was marched whimpering up the stairs where Dad was waiting, armed with a shower nozzle and shampoo.

"Right, get him in the bath, then leave the rest to me."

Mum obeyed instructions and quickly exited the bathroom.

Then all three waited outside with their ears against the door.

"This is for your own good!" said Dad comfortingly, but things rapidly deteriorated. The noises that followed can best be described as sounding like a giant octopus being let loose in the bathtub. The bathroom became filled with splashing, thrashing and squirting noises.

It all ended with a feeble cry of "Let me

out" as Dad finally surrendered.

A barely wet dog leapt from the bathroom, followed by Dad who was soaked from head to toe and covered in foam. As a finishing touch, he had a Mr Whippy-type ice cream swirl of foam on the top of his head.

"Don't say a word," ordered Dad, as he dripped in the doorway. "Perhaps someone could get me a towel."

Mum handed him a towel, then all three of them hurtled downstairs and out into the garden where they almost wet themselves with laughter.

Dad then appeared from the open bathroom window.

"It's not funny," he yelled.

This made them laugh even more.

As a family, they made the decision that it would be worth the expense of taking the dog to the Dog Parlour to be given a once-over, as he really did smell!

They headed into town and parked outside *Bubbly Barkers*.

"What an awful name!" groaned Dad.

"Well, you would know all about bubbles," mumbled Harry.

They were greeted at the doorway by Charlene.

"Oh, what a little treasure," she squeaked in one of those silly voices.

"So what is this little munchkin's name?" she asked.

"Well, we're still working on that one as we've only had him a few days," informed Dad.

"Oh, girls, come over here," she called to two assistants.

"Now what name do we see here?" she cooed.

"Oh, he's a Bobo!" shrieked one.

"No, Scraggy Paws!" declared the other.

"Stop, stop, I've got it, Rambone!" declared Charlene.

"Well, we'll think about all of those," said Dad kindly, desperate to get this over with.

Inside the parlour, a Poodle called Champagne was having her fur dyed pink, a King Charles Spaniel was having a blow dry and, to the astonishment of everyone, a Curly Coated Retriever was actually in curlers!

"I hope you can handle our dog, he's quite lively," said Dad.

"Oh, just look at him, he's an angel," chuckled Charlene.

"Don't worry," she continued, "we've been

washing and grooming dogs for ten years. No dog has ever beaten us yet!"

She then proceeded to list all the services on offer:

Bubbly Barkers

Basic bath and wash	Shave
Oxygen-infused bath	Designer-style perm
Deluxe filtered-water bath	Semi-perm
Standard shampoo	Colour
Deluxe shampoo	Highlights
Seaweed shampoo	Nail clip
De-matt	Ear clean
Coat condition	Gland clean
Towel dry	Flea treatment
Blow dry	Brush
Fluff-up treatment	Condition
Trim	Wax

By this time, the family were dazed!

"Um, just a basic bath and wash, nail clip and towel dry, please," Dad stuttered.

"I think he should have an anal gland clean after the size of the poos he does," whispered Harry.

"Ssh," scowled Mum.

"No problem," beamed Charlene. "Give us two hours and he'll be gleaming!"

The family went off for coffee and cakes at a café in the High Street. No one said much as they ate because they were all nervous about this whole washing and bathing episode. And they had reason to be!

What greeted them when they arrived back at the parlour was like something you see on television.

Two owners were storming out, one with a white Poodle who looked like it had been splatted with purple ink and the other with a Golden Retriever who had certainly been given a designer trim as it resembled a noughts and crosses board!

Inside was a scene of utter devastation. Dog dye covered everything! There was a blue and purple explosion. The floor was like a shampoo ice rink as at least twenty bottles had erupted everywhere.

A Jack Russell sat in one corner on top of a pile of boxes, shivering in terror. In the back

doorway, chained to a rail, stood the dog with no name. As soon as he saw the family, his tail quivered madly and he began to almost dance on tiptoe like a doggy ballerina.

He had a certain look on his face. "What took you so long? Good to see you all at last," it seemed to say.

That was not the look to be found on Charlene's or on her assistants' faces. They emerged looking as if they had been dragged through a pink and purple bog.

Charlene could barely speak.

"Please take him away. We've managed to clean him and there is no charge as long as you never bring him back again!" she managed to mumble.

At this point, one of the assistants, Tiffany, began to sob. As Britney comforted her, she started to sob too.

Dad grabbed the dog and made a hasty exit.

Once in the car, they all burst out laughing hysterically. The dog, however, lay between the two children as usual, wondering what all the fuss was about!

Chapter 10
Dog classes!

In the days that followed, the family and dog began to get to know each other better. They established routines which the dog began to respond to – two meals a day, two walks, sniff at and scratch the door if you want a wee or poo, do not climb on the furniture ... and no begging.

They had given up on trying to stop him scratching the kitchen floor. The grooves were now so deep that the children used them to roll marbles along.

Indoors, there was relative peace and calm, but the garden was another matter.

As had been predicted, the dog did not wee in just one place, and certainly not on the patch they had dug up for him. This had quickly resulted in a lawn that looked as if someone had used a bottle of bleach to create a patchwork design.

Several plants had turned yellow and wilted ... and Mum's rose had died.

The children kept their promise by picking up the poo on a daily basis, apart from on one unfortunate occasion when they had forgotten and Dad stepped in a particularly big pile whilst wearing flip-flops!

However, the biggest problem was the dog's constant desire to dig. Every time he went for a walk, he dug. If not watched carefully, he would dig holes all over the garden. Dad usually kept guard or he sent out the children to keep an eye on him.

"If you get into my vegetable patch, you're back to the Rescue Centre," he regularly warned the dog.

Dad was particularly proud of his vegetable patch and had won *1st prizes* for his vegetables at the County Garden Show. His pride and joy were onions and carrots, while his potatoes were very good too.

This year, he had his best runner beans

ever. In the shed, there
was even a framed photo
of Dad that had appeared
in the local newspaper
holding up his onions!

Mum regularly
reminded Dad that she
was the one that did a
lot of the digging, weeding
and watering, not to mention picking.

"You seem to spend most of your
time simply standing and admiring the
vegetables," she said.

The dog had now stopped pulling when he
walked, so the children had been trusted to
take him out on their own.

Everyone in the street loved him and a
crowd always gathered as he passed by. The
children were so proud of him that they
asked Mum and Dad if they could take him
to Dog Training and Agility classes. These
took place in the Town Hall on Thursdays
and the organisers then regularly entered the

members' dogs into Dog Agility competitions, which the children thought would be great fun.

"No, I don't think so," said Mum. "Remember the dog parlour? He is *not* good with other dogs," she warned.

"Oh, but he's good on walks, he plays with lots of dogs and has never had a fight," pleaded Ella.

"Except with that Pug dog which he just growls at," added Harry.

"I'm not sure," sighed Mum.

"Please," they both pleaded. "It'll improve his behaviour and they might give us tips on how to stop him digging."

"Well, if they do that," interrupted Dad, "I for one will be pleased."

"Well, we'll give it one go but if he plays up, that's it," warned Mum.

"Yeah!" the children cheered.

They could hardly wait for Thursday to arrive and on the day brushed him until he shone like shiny black shoes. The dog could tell something special was happening and seemed to quiver his tail faster than ever!

They walked him proudly to the Town Hall where dogs were already arriving.

"These look a bit classy," said Mum nervously.

"Who cares?" snapped Harry.

In the entrance hall, two ladies sat at a table signing everyone in.

"Hello," said Mum in a posh voice that the children had never heard before.

"Why is she talking in that silly voice?" asked Harry.

"It's a posh dog-owner voice," Ella told him.

The two ladies introduced themselves.

"Hello, I'm Margaret," said one.

"And I'm Evangeline," said the other warmly.

They then suddenly spotted the dog.

"Oh!" they both said together.

"Goodness," said Margaret.

"He *is* rather unusual," Evangeline added quickly.

"There are two Dog Agility clubs in the

town, the other takes place in the Scout Hall," she informed Mum, who by this stage was beginning to go a dark shade of raspberry.

"Well, let's see how we get on here, now that we've walked all this way," said Mum crossly.

Once in the hall, the family realised why they had not received a warm welcome.

Every dog was clearly well bred and if they heard the word 'pedigree' once more, they would scream!

Even the owners appeared to be pedigree, with really posh names like Minty and Clarissa.

There were three men too: Hugo, Adrian and Jasper.

"Why is Hugo wearing …?" Ella tried to ask Harry before being quickly shut up by Mum. (He was wearing a particularly tight-fitting, flamboyant shirt!) A hush came over the hall as everyone suddenly spotted the dog with no name.

Mum was embarrassed so she started to ask everyone what kind of dog they had.

"He's a Lhasa Apso," said one.

"A Tibetan Spaniel," replied another.

"She's a Schnauzer and she's three years old," announced a lady who seemed to be wearing a dress which matched her dog's coat.

Their list went on, Sussex Spaniel, Shih Tzu, Sealyham Terrier ...

Eventually, a tall, silver-haired lady peered over her red glasses and enquired, "And what breed is yours?"

"A Bolognesian Wolfhound!" Mum blurted out before the children had a chance to open their mouths.

No one had heard of such a dog, but none of them wanted to appear stupid so just nodded and said, "Oh!"

"Why did you say that?" asked Harry through gritted teeth.

"It's all I could think of on the spur of the moment. We ate spaghetti Bolognese for tea and you've got some of it down your T-shirt!" Mum whispered back.

The dog owners began to get ready for
the class. Some put their dogs on their laps,
others between their knees, and two ladies
put their Yorkshire Terriers in their handbags!

Suddenly, the doors swung open and in
came the instructor to loud applause.

"Oh no," gasped Mum, "it's Charlene from
the dog parlour."

The two children gasped in horror and
stood opened-mouthed, unable to speak a
word.

This, however, was nothing compared to
Charlene's reaction when she suddenly saw
their dog.

"Help!" she screamed. "Get him away from me, get him away from me," she begged as she backed towards the doors and then flew through them.

After several minutes, during which everyone in the hall whispered to each other and stared at the family, another lady in tartan trousers and a red jumper strode in.

"She looks like a Christmas tree," sniggered Ella.

"Quiet, we're in enough trouble," snapped Mum.

"Good evening, everyone," she said.

"Good evening, Caroline," everyone said in unison. They sounded like children replying at a school assembly.

"Due to unfortunate circumstances," she said, turning towards Mum and the children, "Charlene has been taken ill and is unable to take the class. *I* will, therefore, take the class."

As she uttered the last word, in swept Charlene.

"I'm a professional, I'm a professional. Calm,

97

calm, calm. Breathe, breathe, breathe,"
she muttered.

The lady in red stepped back, allowing
Charlene to take over again.

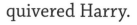

"Right!" said Charlene, with a mean
look on her face. "Let the class begin!" she
announced, looking towards the family.

"She's going to get her revenge,"
quivered Harry.

"She'll pick on us,
Mum," whispered Ella.

"This is doggy hell,"
sighed Mum.

"Now let's begin with a
demonstration from the
wonderful Trixie!" said
Charlene, in a sickly
sweet voice.

"Show us how it should
be done, Tanya, dear,"
she continued.

Out trotted Tanya in
high heels and wearing

the brightest red lipstick ever manufactured, followed obediently by Trixie the Shih Tzu.

First, Trixie walked alongside Tanya as if stuck by superglue to her legs. Then followed a series of 'sits', 'stands' and 'downs'. After that, she proceeded to fetch a variety of objects from a basket and place them perfectly at Tanya's feet.

Finally, she leapt over fences, shot through fabric tunnels and weaved between a row of long poles. Thankfully, she made one tiny mistake by not sitting perfectly at the end.

"Bravo," blubbered Charlene, almost in tears so near perfect was the routine.

Everyone began clapping wildly again.

Tanya trotted smugly back to her place where Trixie was rewarded with three doggy treats and was told she was 'pawgeous'.

"Right, now, *you!*" Charlene snarled, pointing at Mum.

"When I say 'Now'," Mum whispered, "we make a run for it." Before she had a chance to utter a word, the two children took hold of their dog and stepped into the arena.

"We work as a team," said Harry confidently.

Mum covered her eyes, awaiting a disaster.

Then to the astonishment of everyone in the room (most of all Mum and, of course, Charlene), the children completed a perfect agility performance.

The dog sat, stood, lay down and followed the children so closely that he looked like their shadow.

He fetched objects, leapt high over the fences, shot through the tunnel and weaved at such speed around the poles that it made everyone feel dizzy.

The exercise was made complete by a perfect 'Sit' at the end.

The hall echoed to the cheers of everyone, including the other dogs who barked their approval.

Charlene did not join in with this applause as she had fainted and had to be removed from the hall by five committee members.

Everyone gathered around the family, asking them for tips on how to train their dogs.

"A darling, if ever I saw one!" exclaimed Hugo, nearly beside himself with excitement.

The class soon came to an end and as people left, they were informed that no one was to worry about Charlene. She had just had a reaction to the sticky conditions in the hall.

No one did worry and most weren't listening anyway.

"I can't believe it! If I hadn't seen it with my own eyes!" Mum just kept repeating as they walked home,

Once home, Mum rushed in to tell Dad. He'd been working on his vegetable patch. She spoke at such speed that Dad couldn't understand a word she was saying and had to calm her down.

Eventually, both of them turned to the children and asked, "How did you do that?"

"We've been practising on our walks to the fields with him. As soon as we manage to stop him digging, we do lessons!" said Ella proudly.

"But how did you know what to do?" asked Dad.

"We learned from that Crufts Dog Show on the television. Then we watched it again and again on our iPad."

Mum and the children then chatted to Dad late into the evening about what a day they had had, but as it turned out, it wasn't over yet.

Chapter 11
The discovery!

"Right," said Dad, "bedtime. Just look at the time!"

"Where's the dog?" asked Mum. The children whistled.

Nothing. They whistled again. Still nothing.

"The back door's open," yelled Dad, getting up rapidly.

"NO, NO, NO, NOT MY VEGETABLE PATCH!" cried Dad as he reached the back door.

The light from the kitchen shone like a searchlight across an enormous hole where the vegetable patch had once stood.

Sitting on one edge was a grubby dog with very muddy paws. His tail, of course, was quivering happily as ever and in his mouth was the biggest bone the children had ever seen.

Strewn across what was left of the lawn

were shreds of carrot, onion and potato. It was all that remained of Dad's pride and joy of a vegetable patch.

In an effort to calm Dad down, Mum offered the only words she could think of.

"We can start again, darling." This only

made Dad angrier. "It's only a vegetable patch," she foolishly continued. Well, that was it!

"Right, I'm phoning the Dog Rescue Centre, he's going back. I've had enough."

Both children began to cry at this point.

"But we've trained him," pleaded Harry.

"I'll make sure he never does it again," Ella sobbed.

Dad wasn't listening and was marching towards the phone. It was only Mum who managed to stop him by reminding him it was 10 o'clock at night and no one would be at the Centre.

"Well, it will be first thing in the morning, and that's final," insisted Dad.

Even Mum was now crying because she could see the children were so upset. Both were wrapped around the dog, sobbing as he continued to quiver his tail and lick them, totally unaware of the trouble he had caused.

Then Harry suddenly stopped crying and yelled, "Look, quickly come over here."

The whole family stood around the edge of the huge hole and as they peered down, they could see the skeleton of a huge creature.

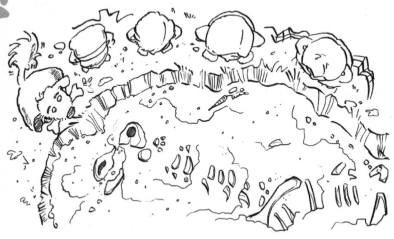

"It's a dragon," gasped Ella.

"No, it's a dinosaur! Our dog has found us a dinosaur!" shrieked Harry, dancing around on the spot.

"Ssh," ordered Dad, "you'll wake the neighbours. And anyway we don't know if it's a dinosaur. It might be a cow or a bull!"

"A cow or a bull? Well, it must be the biggest one in the world!" exclaimed Harry, nearly wetting himself laughing.

"Let's not get overexcited. We'll have to

wait until an expert sees it," said Mum in one of her sensible voices.

"Won't we need to get hold of the bone in the dog's mouth if it's part of the dinosaur?" asked Harry intelligently.

This proved a very difficult task, very difficult indeed.

Firstly, the dog thought it was a game of Chase me, chase me, catch me if you can!

Even four people against a dog proved impossible as when they did manage to corner him, he simply leapt over them.

At one point, Dad got a hand on him and held tight, but he slipped through his arms like a slimy eel.

So it needed a better plan.

"I know," said Mum confidently. She hurried into the house and came out with the dog's favourite biscuits.

The dog took a slight sniff in the air and then gave a look of complete disinterest.

(Well, who'd want a few stingy biscuits when you have a bone that size?)

They then tried tinned food, dried food, even a piece of best steak from the fridge, but nothing tempted him.

"What about a lassoo?" suggested Harry. "Go and get your skipping rope, Ella."

But that dog was as fast as lightning and would have sent any cowboy in the Wild West crazy!

"This is ridiculous," moaned Dad. "Let's just ignore him and eventually he's bound to drop it."

Thirty minutes later, they all gave up and went indoors.

"Wait a minute," said Mum, rushing to the back door. "Walkies," she yelled.

To everyone's amazement and relief, the bone was dropped instantly and the dog hurtled to where his lead was hanging. Clearly nothing meant more to him than a walk!

"As I've said before, Mums know best," she beamed.

Dad took the dog for a quick walk before everyone headed to bed, but not one of them got much sleep as all they could think about was their dinosaur lying beneath the vegetable patch and what might happen the next day.

Everyone woke up early. When Mum and Dad came downstairs, the children were already outside staring into the big hole.

The dog was whining at the back door, banished from the garden to prevent further damage.

"I've been looking in this book," said Harry, sounding like an expert, "and I think it's either a Barapasaurus or a Protoceratops. Here, you look," he beckoned to Ella.

She began to study each page and then compare them to the skeleton. She thought that it could be a Protoceratops, but Harry was probably right with his first guess.

"Yes, it does look like a Barapasaurus," she decided.

"I wish it was a Tyrannosaurus Rex because they are my favourite.

They had 60 teeth, were 40 feet long, 20 feet high, weighed around five to seven tons and had 200 bones," boasted Harry.

Ella began to count the bones she could see at the bottom of the hole, amazed at how much Harry knew.

Harry interrupted her counting by saying, "You can stop counting as they have only been found in Western North America and Mongolia."

"How on earth do you know all of these facts?" she asked.

"I've been up reading all night, I couldn't sleep," he confessed.

Dad had been doing his research too. He had looked on Google and discovered that a dinosaur expert lived in the next town. He contacted him by email. Within a minute of sending his message, the phone rang and an excited caller was on the other end, desperate to come over as soon as possible.

"He's coming over at 11 o'clock," announced Dad excitedly. "He's a professor called

Anthony De Vere," he told the children.

Everyone ate breakfast as fast as they could.

Harry acted as a lookout at the front window, awaiting the professor's arrival.

At exactly 11 o'clock, a silver car pulled up on the drive and a plump man with white hair climbed out. He was wearing glasses, and a jacket and trousers that didn't match. The trouser legs were a little too short for him and you could see he was wearing stripy socks.

He collected a tatty brown case from the back seat of the car and headed for the front door.

"He's here, he's here!" shrieked Harry, making everyone jump and the dog go into a barking fit.

The dog was shut in the front room as they didn't think Professor De Vere would like to be pounced on and licked all over.

Mum brought Professor De Vere in and introduced him to the family.

"Call me Anthony," he said, to stop everyone calling him Professor De Vere.

He didn't want to wait a moment and they all made their way out to the hole.

Professor De Vere (I mean Anthony) gasped and then climbed gingerly into the hole. He opened his case, which was full of useful instruments, including a microscope, trowel, scalpels, little plastic pots and dishes, labels and pens.

Apart from "Well!", "Goodness!" and "Phew!", he said nothing. He just huffed and puffed a lot.

He then took out a long tape measure and noted down at least ten different measurements in a notebook.

After about twenty minutes, he put his hands on his hips and scratched his head.

"I never thought I'd see this day. I can hardly believe it!" he announced.

"What is it, Anthony?" asked Dad.

"I'm almost 99 percent sure that you have uncovered an Iguanodon!" he said.

Even though no one actually knew what that really was, they gasped out loud as Anthony had made it sound so important.

"Is it rare?" asked Harry eagerly.

"It *is* rare, but what makes this amazing is that it is complete. By the looks of it, nearly every bone is in its place. It's as if it just lay down here in your garden 125 million years ago to go to sleep. I've never seen anything like it. It's astonishing," he said, hardly taking his eyes off the dinosaur.

Anthony said he would have to do some further tests and asked if he could come back with some other experts to confirm his conclusions.

As he left, he turned to Harry and Ella and said, "Now remember, this is *your* dinosaur. Whatever happens in the future, your names will go on the *Certificate of discovery*." (Dad had to explain later what that was.)

The children beamed and knew at that moment that Anthony was a good and kind man.

The family sat down in the kitchen in shock.

"An Iguanodon!" they all kept repeating.

If it hadn't been for several deep loud woofs from the front room, they may have sat there all morning.

"The dog!" everyone shouted together.

The dog was so pleased to see them, he nearly knocked them over in his excitement. All thoughts of Dad's vegetable patch were forgotten as this was now a superdog!

The dog was given extra breakfast in his bowl, including two of his favourite bone-shaped biscuits, then taken for one of the longest walks ever!

While they were out, Dad, with the help of poor old Uncle Phil again, built an extra-strong fence around the hole and placed wire netting on the ground to stop the dog digging under.

Later that day, Anthony arrived with two of his dinosaur experts, Clive and Bernard.

Harry noticed that their trousers were also too short and Bernard had a hole in one sock.

Mum told Harry to keep quiet or else!

The three men spent several hours in the hole and Mum and Dad took coffee and biscuits out to them. (Well, except for Bernard. He only drank Fairtrade herbal teas.) So Mum shot down to the local Co-op to get some, and came back with Fairtrade chocolate too.

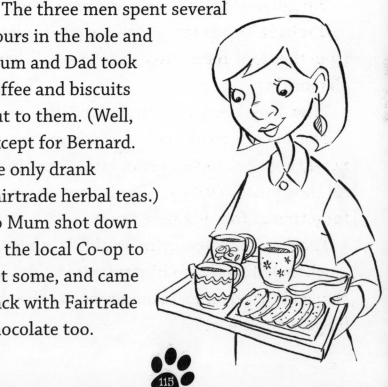

The children sat with the dog on the edge of the hole outside the fence watching each and every thing the men did.

They were using special tools to expose more and more of the dinosaur and were scraping little bits off the bones.

They also kept measuring the bones with special little 'electronic measurers', as Ella called them.

"I can't believe our dog is sitting still for so long," exclaimed Mum.

"It's because he wants one of these bones," replied Harry, "but he's not getting one!"

Just before lunchtime, the men climbed out of the hole.

"There is no doubt about it, this is an Iguanodon and it's the most complete specimen ever found in this country, and possibly the world!" Anthony announced.

The children danced wildly, followed by the dog, who had no idea why they were doing it, but thought it looked fun.

117

Mum and Dad then went into the front room for a chat with Anthony and his colleagues. They closed the door, which meant what he had to say was important and not for children's ears. The children began to get nervous.

"They're going to give the dinosaur to Anthony and we'll never see it again," Ella sighed.

"No, I trust Anthony. Whatever happens, he said that the dinosaur was *ours*," Harry said comfortingly.

Mum, Dad and Anthony came out of the room and there was a lot of hand-shaking. Anthony shook the children's hands too. "Congratulations! This is an amazing discovery," he said.

"I like Anthony," thought Harry again.

Chapter 12
Celebrities!

The rest of the day rushed by like a whirlwind. The telephone rang constantly. Mum and Dad must have had to answer it fifty times or more.

Then Mum told the children to go upstairs and put on their smart clothes.

"Why?" whined Harry, who hated dressing up.

"Just do as you're told!" ordered Mum.

She even made Dad brush his hair. Ella came down the stairs in the dress she had worn at Uncle Phil and Aunty Emma's wedding.

Then the doorbell started ringing, so the dog was put in the front room again.

It was someone from the local newspaper, then people from The *Daily Mail* and *The Guardian*.

When the local BBC and ITV cameras arrived, the children almost went wild with excitement. (Till Mum made one of her faces.)

By now, the back garden was full of people with cameras and they took photos of the dinosaur from every angle. They were allowed to get over the fence, but not in the hole in case they damaged the bones.

Then the family were asked to line up for photos and Harry got really annoyed as Mum kept trying to flatten his hair, which was sticking up.

At last they were ready. Suddenly, Dad yelled, "Stop, stop! The dog. Where's the dog?"

The press people looked confused.

"*We* didn't find the dinosaur, *Digger* did!" explained Dad.

"Who?" asked everyone, including Mum, Harry and Ella.

"Digger, our dog, dug it up," he repeated.

"Well, you must have helped. A dog couldn't dig a hole *that* big," sniggered a spotty-faced young reporter.

"No, Digger dug that hole all by himself!" Dad told them.

"Go and get Digger, children," Dad said.

"Digger?" they both asked.

The family suddenly burst out laughing, realising that they had now found the perfect name for the dog who, for too long now, had had no name.

It took Digger at least half an hour before he was calm enough to be photographed. He had been racing madly around the garden and had licked every reporter and camera person at least twenty times each.

Eventually, Mum put a lead on him and endless photos were taken of Digger and his family.

The following day was even more exciting as they all appeared on breakfast TV.

Thanks to all the training the children had been doing, Digger sat when told and behaved

himself, apart from knocking over a coffee cup with his quivering tail and cocking his leg and weeing over a TV camera stand!

The family had one of the best days imaginable. The television staff were so kind and everyone fell in love with Digger.

They were given a tour of the studios and met some famous people. They even saw where the news was read from.

But as the family returned home, they were in for one more big surprise!

As they turned into their street, they were greeted by a huge crowd who had put up banners saying 'Well done, Digger!', 'Digger, dynamic dinosaur dog!', 'Digger, we love you!' and other nice things.

The house was covered with balloons and bunting and all the family's friends were there.

Everyone wanted to pat Digger and have a photo taken with him.

Digger loved the attention and his tail quivered, quivered and quivered some more.

The town councillors and the mayor came too. But the trio who put the icing on the cake were Charlene, Tiffany and Britney. They arrived carrying a huge bone and balloons.

All three were wearing pink tops with *Bubbly Barkers* on the front and *Bubbles* on the back.

"Hi, it's us," squealed Charlene, waving frantically. "Where's the little angel?"

Digger took one look at her and hid behind Mum.

"Look, little Diggerpoos. I've got a bone for little dumpling," she continued.

The bone had a pink ribbon tied around it and did look delicious to a dog. So Digger finally gave into temptation and snapped it out of her hands.

"Oh, the little treasure," she whispered. "Now, please make sure you bring back this little star to *Bubbly Barkers*," she pleaded, making sure she said "*Bubbly Barkers*" as loud as possible.

"He can have free washes for life," she added.

Mum was just about to give her a mouthful in reply when Dad stopped her and whispered, "Just imagine the fun we'll have each time Digger visits. And for free!"

So Mum said nothing and Dad thanked Charlene for the kind offer.

Little by little, the crowd dispersed after everyone had photographed and patted Digger at least once. He gripped his bone throughout, determined not to lose this one.

As the family finally went indoors, Mum picked up the post and they all collapsed into the kitchen. They sat around the table and drank hot chocolate. While reflecting on their amazing day, Mum gave the children two *hand delivered* letters addressed to them.

Inside the first envelope was a letter from Anthony De Vere.

"You read it to us, Dad, as it looks really important and I want to take every bit in," asked Ella.

In the letter, Anthony asked the children if their dinosaur could be carefully lifted by archaeologists and then reconstructed and put on display in a national museum. He went on to say that by being in a museum, people from all over the world could see it.

He finished by telling them that even though it would be looked after by the museum, they would always own it and could visit for free for the rest of their lives. (Which they did do, and in later years took their own children and grandchildren.)

Ella turned to Harry and said, "Remember you told me you trusted Professor De Vere? Well, I do too."

So they agreed right there and then.

"What about the other envelope?" Mum reminded Dad.

He opened it and inside was the *Certificate of discovery*. It confirmed the time and the place of discovery, but the name of the discoverer was left blank. A Post-it note was attached to it from Anthony.

"You decide which names should go on the certificate," it said.

The family looked at each other.

"DIGGER!" they all exclaimed.

But Digger was much too busy chomping on his bone and thinking about his next digging adventure to notice!